Paper Heart

Paper Heart

Aileen Arrington

FRONT STREET
Asheville, North Carolina

Library of Congress Cataloging-in-Publication Data
Arrington, Aileen.
Paper heart / Aileen Arrington.—1st ed.
p. cm.
Summary: Sixth-grader Nadia begins to defy her overprotective
mother, hoping to be seen as more than the "poor sick girl" who
cannot participate in school activities, form friendships, or even
be outside in the cold for fear she has inherited her father's heart trouble.
ISBN-13: 978-1-932425-61-1 (hardcover : alk. paper)
[1. Heart murmurs—Fiction. 2. Sick—Fiction. 3. Mothers and daughters—Fiction.
4. Schools—Fiction. 5. Self-perception—Fiction.] I. Title.
PZ7.A743365Pap 2006
[Fic]—dc22
2006000798

FRONT STREET
An Imprint of Boyds Mills Press, Inc.
A Highlights Company
815 Church Street
Honesdale, Pennsylvania 18431

In memory of my father

The secret was hidden in plain sight,

but finding it would take some time.

After all, Nadia did not even know

she was looking for it.

| one |

Nadia stood alone under a giant oak at the edge of the school grounds. The icy wind cut at her face. She pushed her dark hair inside the hood of her coat and pulled the drawstrings tight. Her eyes watched everything, gray eyes the color of the cold winter sky with dark circles under them that made the gray look even lighter.

Because of her bad heart, Nadia did not play at recess. It was a wonder she was outside at all. Usually she stayed inside on days like this.

Across the grounds, the massive schoolhouse stood at the top of a small rise like a brick castle in a grove of oaks, and behind her tree, the ground dropped away to a fence that separated her from the railroad tracks. Sometimes trains went by, and Nadia wished she were on them going anywhere, as long as it was away from that schoolyard.

The other sixth graders scurried around, murmuring, screaming, and so far as they were concerned, Nadia did not exist.

But Nadia didn't care. What were they to her? Who cared about them and their stupid games?

Maybe Mama's plan would be for the best. Take her out of school. Home-school her. Have her do her lessons at Mama's little real-estate office in town, even though she did hate that secretary who worked there.

Then no one Nadia's age would know there was a Nadia.

And maybe she would go ahead and disappear altogether. She felt like she was almost gone now, standing there under her tree.

two

A play? It excited Nadia. Just the idea. Not that she could be in a play, not her. But the idea!

After recess, Mrs. Riley, who was little and round and old, had gone to the board still in her coat and written the words *Christmas Play*. Nadia waited at her desk, her eyes stuck on the words.

She told herself she didn't care. Not really. She put her head down on her desk and waited anyway, to hear Mrs. Riley talk about it. Mrs. Riley didn't appear to worry when Nadia did that, so Nadia lay there until her arm went to sleep. By the time Mrs. Riley got her coat off, she seemed to have forgotten all about the words on the board, and she gave the class their Friday writing assignment instead. "Write about something you do for fun," she said.

Nadia got out her paper. She wished she could put that she was an actress. Then she'd be something.

The Actress, by Nadia
This actress is in real plays with real live grown actors. They are in a town where you have to drive about an hour to get there. You might be surprised

*to know that this actress is me. My mother lets me
be in plays because I can't do tiring things that take
exercise, but I do not mind because it is a lot more
fun anyway.*

Nadia looked at her classmates. They all knew that
the sick girl would not be in their play. Now they'd see
that she couldn't care less about their old stupid school
play.

Nadia had read in a magazine about a girl who played
Helen Keller.

*I had a part in a play called <u>The Miracle Worker</u>
where I played a blind girl. Plus deaf too. I was the
star.*

Nadia erased the last sentence. They might get mad
and think she was bragging.

Not that she could use this paper. That would be
wrong. Nadia got a new sheet and tried to think of something else while she glanced around at the other girls. A
bunch of them took dance. They'd be writing about their
recital. It was all they talked about at lunch every day.

"Who wants to share?" asked Mrs. Riley. One of the
dancers got up to read. Nadia was right. It was all about
the recital. Then a boy read about his dog, and another
about his baseball team. Nadia still had nothing on her
new sheet of paper when her hand just sort of went up by

itself, and she found herself standing beside her desk and reading the actress paper.

"My! I didn't know that," said Mrs. Riley. "In Florence there's a place called the Little Theatre. Is that the group you're in?"

Nadia didn't know what the Little Theatre was. She looked at Mrs. Riley. "Yes?" she said.

The teacher smiled, and Nadia sat down. She could tell. They were thinking about her. They were watching. No more "poor sick girl" looks, either. This was different.

I *am* different now, Nadia thought.

 | three |

Nadia got tired of listening to the others read their papers. She put her head back down on her desk and kept it there until Mrs. Riley started talking.

"Now quiet down, class," Mrs. Riley began in her slow way. She shifted her weight and fumbled through a pile of papers on her desk. "I have an announcement here ... somewhere," she said. She gave a little sigh and glared at the papers. "As you might know, sixth grade will be doing the Christmas program this year at the PTA. Our class is doing a play."

Nadia sat up tall. She loved plays. And play-acting. She acted out stories at home all the time with her paper dolls. And a *real* play. It made her insides quiver.

And though no teacher had ever even halfway considered letting Nadia be in a play, Nadia found it fun to watch the other kids practice, and fun to watch the play, and fun to pretend. And besides, if Mrs. Riley believed her paper ...

She looked at the other students. Who would Mrs. Riley choose?

"I have the parts here"—Mrs. Riley stopped and disappeared behind her desk to lift her large purse off the floor—"if I can just put my hands on them." She rummaged through the purse. "Aha." She laughed and pulled out a set of papers.

"Well now, children." Mrs. Riley took a deep breath and adjusted her glasses on the end of her nose. "I guess the first thing we'll need to do is have tryouts. Come get a copy of the first act if you're interested."

Nadia sat still and watched the children swarming to Mrs. Riley's desk.

Tryouts?

This time the teacher was going to let everyone *try out*? Not just pick kids herself? This time *she, Nadia, sick girl,* stood a chance?

Did Mrs. Riley know she made that up about the actress? If she went and got one of those copies, would Mrs. Riley say, *No, Nadia, not you*?

Nadia crept to the teacher's desk and grabbed the last copy. The radiators made a knocking sound, like Nadia's heart. She took deep breaths to calm down, like Mama had told her.

Mrs. Riley wrote the homework assignment on the board, and Nadia sat down and put her palms flat on her tryout paper. She breathed in and made a little *o* with her lips and let her breath out slowly. Calmly. Like Mama said.

This was her chance. She would learn the lines.

She had all weekend. She would be ready on Monday. She would do better than all the other kids. Then, the night of the play, Mama would change her mind about Nadia. Everyone would. And Mama would want her in more plays, not in home school.

Nadia looked out the window. Blackbirds soared in and lit on bare branches against the gray sky. Nadia felt nervous. Mama had said home school would be perfect for her. So much easier on her. Even when she told Mama she wanted to go to regular school, Mama said Nadia felt that way because the idea was new. That lots of kids loved home school, and she would too.

But everything was changing. Or would be. When Mama saw this play.

She *had* to win the part.

After all, this was her last chance ever to be in a play. Soon, in January, Mama would start home school for Nadia. But when Mama saw her in this play, then maybe—surely—Mama would drop the home-school idea.

| four |

On her way out of school, Nadia stopped to look into the auditorium. At the front hallway of the school, two sets of double doors served as entrances. Inside, the aisles sloped through the rows of audience chairs to the stage, where the wooden floor shone, waxed and gleaming. Heavy curtains hung to the sides.

Once, when she was in Girl Scouts, Nadia had stood on that stage, before Mama had decided Scouts was not good for her. She remembered it now, the way the dark was broken by the stage lights, and she remembered the soft clicking sound of her new shoes as she walked across those gleaming old planks. She had loved those shoes.

Soon now, she'd be back up there where she belonged. After she'd won the tryouts.

Nadia hurried down the hall to the side entrance and out toward the car that waited for her. It should have been snow, she thought when she saw the drizzle. It was so cold. But it didn't snow much in South Carolina. Still, Mama would be terrified if she knew her frail child was out in this. Nadia ducked back inside and tied her hood securely. She clutched her book bag with the tryout parts in it and hurried to the car.

Most days the secretary from the real-estate business picked her up and took her to Mama's office, where Mama would have a snack waiting for her and she would do her homework. Once she had taken her paper dolls to play with at the office, and the secretary had remarked with surprise that a big girl like her was playing with paper dolls. Nadia had hated her ever since.

"How was your day?" Mrs. Branch asked. As always.

"Fine."

"Fine?" Mrs. Branch seemed a little taken aback. Usually Nadia said something negative.

Nadia looked out the window. She wasn't telling about the play. Not now. Not to Mrs. Branch. She would tell Mama tonight after supper. Mama would probably start helping her learn the lines then. Nadia could always talk Mama into fun things, like playing cards or a board game.

Mrs. Branch turned the car around. Nadia looked back at the children who were still on the school grounds, and started picking out some friends. After she got popular, all the kids would want to be her friend.

Nadia, not so sick anymore.

Nadia, talented actress.

Nadia, popular girl.

| five |

When Nadia was five years old, she learned three things. She learned that Daddy had gone away and was never coming back. She learned that she was not supposed to talk about him. And she learned that if she was not very careful, she too might go away and never come back.

No one said it in exactly those words, but Nadia learned it just the same.

Nadia lived with her mother twelve miles from town in the middle of the woods in a two-hundred-year-old house with peeling paint and a yard full of enormous japonica bushes and gigantic oaks draped with Spanish moss and twining wisteria vines that burst out amazing purple in the spring. Mama said the house was too big and empty, but Nadia liked it. So they did not move.

When Nadia got home that day, she curled up on the couch beside Mama, and Mama read aloud from a book. Nadia loved the books Mama chose. "Can we read more after supper?" Nadia asked when Mama put the book down.

Mama smiled. "I want to see what happens too," she said, "but tonight I've got some paperwork from the office."

"Noooo," Nadia whined. "Let's read more." She followed Mama to the kitchen with the book in her hand. She ran her finger over the picture on the cover. She knew she was acting spoiled, but Mama would let her get away with anything. After all, she had a bad heart.

"I'll be cutting back on my work in January," Mama said. "We'll have lots more time for books then."

Nadia and Mama had supper in the little kitchen. The gas space heater flickered from the old fireplace it was tucked into. They ate in the kitchen on cold nights. The dining room was too chilly in winter.

Nadia pulled at her ponytail and tried to braid it. She had picked at her supper, what she wanted of it.

"Mrs. Riley told us there's going to be a play for the PTA meeting. She gave us all papers. You have to try out."

"Stop playing with your hair, Nadia. Finish your milk."

Nadia dropped the ponytail and took one swallow of her chocolate milk. "There's going to be a *play*, Mama!"

"Well, you don't want any part of that," Mama said.

What? Nadia hadn't expected that.

Mama's eyes fixed on her daughter. "She's not making you *all* try out, is she?"

Nadia looked away. "No. Just if you want to."

Why hadn't she realized? Mama would not want her in the play. Mama would think it would be too much of a strain on her.

"Nadia?" Mama said. "Why aren't you eating? Are you feeling all right?"

Nadia picked up her fork and poked at her hominy. "There's no cheese."

Mama got up and went to the refrigerator for cheese. She put it in front of Nadia. "You have to eat. You have to keep your strength up."

Nadia took a cheese slice and picked it apart into tiny pieces, spacing them evenly in her hominy. She ate only the parts of the hominy that had cheese in them.

The wind shook the old window in its loose-fitting frame. Nadia felt an icy stream of air sneak in and touch her face. Mama would not ruin the play. Not if she didn't know Nadia was in the play. It would be a surprise. It would have to be a surprise.

She wouldn't tell Mama, but she would try out. Then Mama couldn't say no. Mama hadn't really said no.

Nadia studied the birds in the pattern on the edge of her plate. She put her finger on one. The blue birds. Her father had told her the story of those birds once. Those birds used to be people, and they had been changed into birds so they could fly away and be free.

| six |

When Nadia was eight, the paper dolls had arrived in a box as a Christmas present from Aunt Amy in Tennessee. Nadia didn't much like them. They lay in their box for years until one day she found them and changed her mind.

She pulled the box out of her closet and sat cross-legged in the middle of her bed. *For ages 7–10*, it said on the box. Nadia was too old for the dolls now, according to the toymakers. But what did they know?

After all, other girls her age didn't have heart trouble. Other girls her age could have real girls at the house. Or play outside with their brothers and sisters. So it was okay to play with paper dolls, even if she was too old.

Nadia opened the box and pulled out the dolls one by one, placing them in a line in front of her. She would let the paper dolls put on the play. She would learn the part of Christina. It was the best part in the play. Whoever played Christina would be the star. It was the part for her. It was the longest part, but she knew she could learn it.

It was past her bedtime when Nadia put the dolls back in the box. She was hiding the tryout paper inside her schoolbook when Mama came to the door. "Are you working on homework?"

"We've got a test next week," Nadia said. She hadn't meant to lie, but this was new. Keeping secrets from Mama. Besides, she thought, what she said was kind of true. A test to see who was best for each part.

"I'll talk to Mrs. Riley about this," Mama said. "You have to have your rest."

"I'm *through*," Nadia said. She frowned and threw the book down on her bedside table. "I was just reading. I didn't … I didn't have to study. You don't have to talk to Mrs. Riley, Mama." Now her voice was whiny. She knew she was acting like a brat again. Aunt Lela would tell Mama not to put up with it. But Nadia didn't care. Besides, Aunt Lela didn't know about the play.

Nadia curled up in her long flannel nightgown under the pile of covers and pulled the blanket up around her neck. "I *don't* want you to talk to Mrs. Riley!"

"Okay, then. You have a good night," Mama said. She kissed Nadia on the top of her head and shut off the light. Nadia watched Mama stop outside the door and glance back. "Good night, Nadia," Mama said again.

"Don't call her!" Nadia said.

She lay back and stared into the darkness at forms coming into view, like when Mama took her to the movies and the lights went out before the film started.

Nadia liked to act out the stories from the movies. She acted them out with the paper dolls. She didn't have any real friends because she couldn't play like other kids, and Mama didn't think she should have anyone over at the house. Regular children played too rough and wild, running around and all, and she couldn't do that. Because of her heart, she couldn't do that.

Mama had tried inviting kids over, but it hadn't turned out well. Nadia always ended up trying to join in some game that required running or jumping, and Mama would come and stop the game, and Nadia would be embarrassed.

The paper dolls were in their box now. She couldn't see their smiling faces. But she knew they weren't smiling. They were frowning.

| seven |

The bicycle was soft gray. Silvery gray, the sales clerk told her, and it had a little button that made a bell ring when you pushed it. But Mama was upset when she found Nadia there, stopped in the store, that Saturday, her eyes bright and hopeful. Mama was mad when the salesman told her it was just the right bike for Nadia. "Matches those eyes," he said, all smiles.

"You don't understand," Mama explained to him. "My daughter has a bad heart." She pulled Nadia away as the salesman looked embarrassed and mumbled he was sorry, he didn't mean any harm, and Nadia felt sorry for the man and angry with Mama. She knew why Mama did what she did, but she was angry all the same.

Mama took Nadia to the girls' department and bought her a beautiful blue sweater. The sweater was lovely, and she felt pretty when she wore it. But it wasn't the bike.

Nadia wore her new blue sweater on Monday morning for her tryout. She sat at breakfast, picking at her oatmeal. She didn't like oatmeal. She felt cross, and it showed in her voice. "Can't I ride the bus to school?"

She knew what Mama would say. Mama had said it before. "No, Nadia."

Nadia put her spoon down. Then she would not eat any more. *Why?* she wanted to say. But did not say. She knew the answer.

It's too long a ride on a bus. Those children are too rough. There could be a fight, and you're not strong enough to stand up for yourself. You know that, Nadia.

Nadia tightened her lips and pushed her bowl away. She was tired of Mama saying no.

Mama does not want me to be in the play.

But Nadia would not think about that.

So Mama drove Nadia into town to school, not realizing that Nadia had been practicing the lines all weekend when Mama thought she was reading or playing with her paper dolls, and they waited in the car for the bell, watching from behind the protective glass of the window. Mama handed Nadia a note: *Mrs. Riley, Nadia may not play outdoors today.* Nadia watched the other kids running and standing and clapping hand games and jumping rope, their noses red in the cold, and all the time Nadia wished she could be out there and not inside the car. Out in that fresh, icy air.

A little flock of birds spun toward a hickory tree and lit on the branches, dark against the white-gray sky. The bell. The birds rushed off in the wind again, and Nadia hurried to get out of the car. "Slow down!" Mama said.

So Nadia said good-bye to Mama and walked slowly to the end of her line to go inside on tryout day while the quivery feeling in her stomach grew and grew. But it was a good quivery feeling.

Nadia knew the lines.

Nadia was ready.

| eight |

There. On the little bulletin board at the front of the class. Nadia saw it when she came into the room. *Tryout Sign-up List*. Other kids were there already. Names were on the list.

Nadia rushed to her desk and grabbed her pencil and went back. Her eyes flew over the words on the page. *Girls' parts. Christina*. The best part. The star.

Her part.

But there were already names there. Other girls wanted that part too. Including Patsy.

Nadia had forgotten all about her.

Patsy, with her big brown eyes and her little junior Snow White looks. Patsy, always in school shows. And Patsy was very good in the shows. And all the kids and all the teachers knew it.

Patsy would win the part. The teachers always picked her.

Nadia frowned. Not this time. She wrote her name in the blank under Patsy's. As she turned, she bumped into Patsy.

"*You* signed up for Christina?" Patsy said.

"*Yes.*"

Nadia didn't mean to sound mad. But she realized she did. She *was* mad. And she felt sick. Maybe she should go to the sick room. Maybe this whole idea was wrong. Mama would think it was wrong.

Mrs. Riley shifted around at her desk. She was going to stand up. She was going to get the list.

Nadia's heart raced. She would ask to go to the sick room! She pushed past Patsy and sat down and raised her hand. The nurse would call her mother. The thought made her feel better. She took a deep breath and slowly blew it out.

Mrs. Riley looked at Nadia's hand waving in the air. "Nadia, you may go first," she said.

Nadia put her hand down. *First?* she thought. *But I want to go to the sick room.*

Nadia reconsidered. Maybe she didn't need the nurse. Patsy had her perfect little Snow White nose sticking in the air and a confident smile on her lips.

She makes me sick, thought Nadia. She stood up and walked to the front of the room. Her stomach felt wiggly. Her heart flopped around too hard. Her head felt squirmy. Visions of Patsy twirled in her eyes. She could ask to go see the nurse right this minute.

But this is my only chance, and I can say those lines perfectly.

| nine |

It was magic.

At first Nadia felt shaky, and she thought she might have to lie down right there on the floor. Then she remembered the first line of the Christina part. She said it, and then she felt fine. Just like that. Like being at home in her room practicing with the paper dolls. And it was so much fun she almost laughed when it was over. She looked at Mrs. Riley.

Mrs. Riley was smiling.

The class began to clap.

"Why, that was outstanding, Nadia," Mrs. Riley said. "Just excellent! I did not realize what an amazing little actress you are."

Nadia went back to her desk, beaming and feeling pleased with herself and not at all embarrassed by the applause.

It was a new feeling. She wasn't so different from the other kids. She could be important too. She knew she had won that part. She was a natural actress. A sickly little thing like her … had won.

Four other girls tried out for the same part. Louise stumbled over some lines, forgot several of them and had to be prompted by Mrs. Riley. Margaret didn't sound natural, and Irene got the giggles.

Patsy went last. First she informed Mrs. Riley that she was a dancer. "Tap and ballet, and modern jazz. My mother says I am good enough to be a professional dancer, and when I get to be a teenager I am going to New York to study dance. I might be performing at Lincoln Center, and maybe on Broadway too, or Radio City Music Hall, as a Rockette."

"Well, that is very interesting," Mrs. Riley told Patsy. "But you can go ahead and recite the lines for this play now."

Patsy did pretty well.

But I did the best, Nadia decided. And she figured Mrs. Riley felt the same, because all Mrs. Riley said to Patsy was "That was nice."

The tryouts for the leading boy's role were next. Then Mrs. Riley said they would have to get some work done, and they would do the other parts that afternoon. Then she would decide who got the parts. She would let them know tomorrow.

Tomorrow? She had to wait for tomorrow for Mrs. Riley to tell everyone that she won the part? Nadia wanted her to say it now.

"But," Mrs. Riley told them, "you will all be in the program. Mrs. Beckley is in charge of the chorus, and you'll be in that if you don't get a part. And the chorus," she added, "is very important."

Nadia looked around, a little frown on her face.

The chorus was *not* important. And she did not want to be in it. She had been in a chorus before, and it wasn't anything.

Mrs. Riley put the math assignment on the board. Nadia ran her fingers back and forth through the little hollowed-out pencil tray in her desk. Her fingers came out gray and shiny with graphite, and she tried to rub it off in her math book. A good deal came off, leaving dark smudges on the division problems. She thought about her tryout. It *was* excellently outstanding. Just like Mrs. Riley had said.

Unless.

Unless Mrs. Riley was just being nice because she was the sick girl?

And then old Patsy had tried out. The teachers always chose Patsy.

Nadia started feeling sick again. She put her head down on her desk and spent some more time looking at her smudgy gray fingertips.

She tried to rub the gray off. It wouldn't all come off, so some of it must be her skin tone. Grayish skin. That was bad. Suddenly she felt sick to her stomach. Why was her skin getting that color? She got up from her desk and started toward Mrs. Riley, but she tripped in the aisle on her book bag. The fall hurt.

"Nadia!" Mrs. Riley said, starting toward her. The pain in Nadia's knee made her feel nauseated. Someone was trying to help her up.

"How do you feel?" Mrs. Riley asked.

Nadia was crying now. "I don't feel good. I feel awful," she cried. "I want Mama. Call my mother. I need to see the doctor!" She couldn't breathe right. She didn't remember ever feeling this bad. The girls who had picked her up were holding her arms. The pain in her knee was searing.

"Take her to the nurse," Mrs. Riley said.

"Call my mother," Nadia cried. Loudly. Too loudly. The room was so quiet, except for her. She felt ashamed. She had never heard the room so quiet. They must know she was awfully sick this time. Her heart was beating hard. Some girl was giggling softly. Now they thought she was a crybaby. Well, she didn't care about them. That mean old girl. "I can't breathe," she yelled. "You have to call my mother!" Mrs. Riley was helping the girls get her out the door. They all took her to the nurse.

"She tripped and hurt her knee pretty bad," Mrs. Riley said. "I'm going to call her mother. Just to be on the safe side. She does have the heart condition, you know."

Nadia lay on the cot in the sick room. The school nurse checked her blood pressure. By the time Mama arrived, Nadia felt fine, but Mama took her by Doc Smith's anyway. Then Nadia spent the rest of the day in Mama's office with an ice pack on her knee, thinking.

Why did she have to act like that? Get all panicky and scared like that. Now she realized it had just been her knee. Not her heart. Why was she such a big baby?

In front of the whole class. She bet none of them acted like that.

But they'd sure change their mind about her when she got the part. When she starred in the play. They'd all admire her then. They'd be in awe of her. Like some movie star. They'd forget all about her acting like a fool then.

| ten |

When the wind was icy and the sky was slate and the birds sat in long rows on the telephone wires, Nadia waited in the car with Mama for the bell to ring. Tuesday morning. Like so many mornings waiting in the car. But so different. Nadia would not miss this day at school. She had told Mama her sore knee didn't hurt at all.

She watched the girls jumping rope. Patsy was jumping, and she was a good jumper. She was even on a double-dutch jumping team.

Nadia could hear the rope popping and the girls' words snapping. She said them too. "Tell me—who will— marry me. Rich man—poor man—beggar man—thief."

The rope stopped. Patsy missed. The girls shouted, "Thief!" and Nadia laughed.

"You're mighty excited this morning," Mama said.

"School's gonna be fun today," Nadia said.

"What's up?" Mama asked.

Nadia closed her lips tight. She wanted to say, *Today Mrs. Riley will announce that I won the part!* But Mama mustn't know yet. Nadia smiled. They'd go to the PTA. Nadia would go to help backstage and then she'd walk onto the stage as the star. Mama would be amazed.

"What's so much fun today?" Mama asked again.

Nadia picked at her book bag. It had to be a secret. "Nothing," she said. The bell rang, and she almost stumbled out of the car.

"Slow down, Nadia," Mama called.

Nadia didn't want to slow down. She felt like flying over to the line and running up the steps and finding out *now* that she had the part, but she walked slowly and deliberately, as usual, and stood at the back of the line. A cold gray mist cloaked the school grounds. Nadia put her hood up and watched Mama's car, still waiting at the edge of the playground, waiting until she was in the building. Maybe Mrs. Riley had already written her name on the board as the winner.

No one's name was on the board. Mrs. Riley took roll, and Nadia waited some more. Waited to be announced as Christina.

"We'll go to the auditorium at eleven o'clock to run through the play," Mrs. Riley said. "I'll announce the parts now. Those with speaking parts can practice together in the back of the room or out in the hall until then."

Patsy leaned out into the aisle with some of her friends, and they whispered.

Nadia glared at them. Patsy expected the part, of course, considering she always got everything she wanted. She would be mad at Nadia when Nadia won.

But I was the best, Nadia thought. *I know I was. So Patsy will just have to get over it.*

She folded her hands on her desk and waited, watching Mrs. Riley, looking as unsuspecting as she could, even though she knew what Mrs. Riley knew. She was the winner.

"Some of you did not get the part you tried out for," Mrs. Riley was saying, "but you will be given an important smaller part. We couldn't have a play without these other parts." Mrs. Riley fumbled through her papers on the desk. Impatience quivered just under Nadia's skin.

"The part of Father will be played by David," Mrs. Riley said.

The children clapped, and some girls giggled. David nodded in a goofy way. Nadia laughed. He was cute. It would be fun to be in the play with him.

"And the part of Mother will be played by Janet."

Janet turned red and put her hands over her face. The class clapped again and stared at her.

"The children will be played by Clarence, Wendell, and Bethy," Mrs. Riley continued.

Nadia picked at her thumbnail. She wrapped her arms around herself. Not long now.

"The part of Christina, the first visitor of Christmas—" Mrs. Riley continued.

A beam burst onto Nadia's face. She couldn't help it. It was going to be so much fun!

"—will be played by Patsy."

| eleven |

A draining numbness. All the feelings drained down, down. Away. She didn't even hear the applause for Patsy, just Mrs. Riley's words again. Banging around in her mind. Banging around the room. *Will be played by Patsy. By Patsy? Patsy.*

Her part. Patsy would play her part.

Nadia was vaguely aware of Patsy smiling, turning to look at the clapping children, a miniature Snow White waving to the dwarfs … only they weren't dwarfs. They were her classmates, and they should have been mad that the best actress did not win. Weren't they tired of Princess Patsy?

Nadia realized that her mouth was hanging open, so she closed it. She should be clapping too. She didn't want to look like a sore loser. But her arms felt weak, and by the time she lifted them to join the others, Mrs. Riley had already announced that the part of the second visitor would go to Grainger.

Suddenly Nadia sensed that no one noticed her being a sore loser. No one noticed her at all. They had gone right back to thinking of her the way they always had. They'd all forgotten what a good job she had done. After all, they were all expecting Patsy to get the part. Didn't she always? So they'd forgotten whose tryout was the best. And they had put Nadia back in her "sick girl" box.

Nadia put her hands on her desk and stared straight at Mrs. Riley. Mrs. Riley was so unfair. Patsy was just the teacher's pet. Or maybe Mrs. Riley didn't think she, Nadia, could do anything because she was sickly. Maybe it was the way she looked. Her skinny-armed self and the dark circles under her eyes. But hadn't she proven with the tryout that she was good? Didn't Mrs. Riley *remember*? Or did she just not care?

Tears stung at Nadia's eyes, but she blinked hard and they didn't fall, and then she realized that Mrs. Riley had finished all the announcements and she hadn't really been listening. Did Mrs. Riley give her one of the small parts? Surely she got one of those. But she didn't hear Mrs. Riley say her name. Maybe she missed it, though.

She saw the children whose names had been called crowding around Mrs. Riley's desk to get their copies of the whole play.

And she waited, knowing that surely someone would call her up there to get her small part. Someone would remind her.

But no one did.

Should she go up there and look at the list and see where her name was? Which one of the small parts she got? A small part would be something. A small part would be fun. Not as much fun as the lead, but fun.

Nadia slipped out of her seat and approached the children at the front. She looked at Mrs. Riley. Mrs. Riley didn't seem to notice her. Nadia looked for a list. There it was. She didn't see her name anywhere, though. She went back to her desk and sat down. She blinked back the tears.

Mrs. Riley didn't even give her a little part? She hated Mrs. Riley. She had thought Mrs. Riley was nice. But now she knew. Mrs. Riley was mean and unfair and prejudiced against a sickly child. And in favor of Little Miss Teacher's Pet that all the teachers liked because of her pink cheeks, and her eyes that didn't have dark circles under them, and her Snow White looks and … and because she was going to be a famous dancer and …

Mrs. Riley was bad.

| twelve |

The children who had parts went out into the hall, and Mrs. Riley said the others should work on their math. So unfair again. Why should they have to work when the players got to do the play? It was mean. And she deserved that part. It should have been hers.

Well, she wouldn't do the math. If that's what Mrs. Riley thought of her, that she was just some sickly kid who couldn't do anything, then she'd be sickly. She put her head down on her desk and waited. She knew what would happen, and it did.

"Mrs. Riley, Mrs. Riley," some girl was saying. It sounded like June. "Nadia's sick. She's got her head down."

And sure enough, Mrs. Riley asked her if she needed to go to the nurse, and she sat up and nodded. She had done this a million times before.

"Maybe you'd better go with her," Mrs. Riley said to June. So June went with Nadia out by the kids in the hall. They were cutting up and laughing. And Patsy was saying a line wrong. Wrong!

Nadia stopped and stared at Princess Patsy. Defiantly.

"What are you looking at?" Patsy said.

Nadia didn't know what to say to that, so she went to the water fountain. She usually didn't stop for water. Usually she really felt sick.

At the clinic, Nadia went to the familiar cot and lay down. June sat beside her. June hadn't gotten a part either—probably not smart enough to learn the words. Everyone knew that. But June was nice.

"You need to go back to class, June," the nurse said.

Actually it wasn't the real nurse. Nadia didn't recognize this one.

"And what seems to be the problem?"

This lady didn't know her as the one with the bad heart. Nadia decided on a stomachache.

"Well, I'll just let you lie there a while and we'll see if it doesn't get better soon."

Nadia lay there and fumed. Then she felt bored. She sat up. "Can I go get my library book?" she asked.

"You must be feeling better," said the lady.

Nadia sat quietly.

"Are you?" asked the lady. "Are you feeling a little better now?"

Nadia shrugged her shoulders.

"Do you think you can go back to your class?"

Nadia stood up. "Yes." After all, she did want to be there before the class left for the auditorium at eleven o'clock. She wanted to go too, and watch the kids practice, even if it wasn't her. She liked plays. She liked the auditorium. They hardly ever got to go there. It would be better than this.

Everyone was coming back in the room from the hall at ten-thirty when Nadia got back. There were more copies of the play on Mrs. Riley's desk. They were extra. "Can I have one of these?" Nadia asked.

Mrs. Riley smiled at her. "Of course," she said.

Nadia looked back at Mrs. Riley with a blank expression, and took the crisp, newly printed play to her book bag. Maybe she would let the paper dolls put on the whole play.

| thirteen |

When Nadia was little, she sat on the curb at Vacation Bible School alone and watched the others jumping and running in the green and blue and yellow June mornings. She sat with her butter cookie and cup of purple Kool-Aid that the Sunday-school ladies had made, and she always made it last as long as she could so that when the others asked her to play, she could say she wasn't through with her snack.

Now she didn't make excuses. They all knew. Now they left her alone. They didn't quite know what to do with her, but the day the parts were announced, they elected her class vice president.

The class had been studying government. First they elected a president. Then someone thought of Nadia for vice president. If they thought for one minute that being class vice president made up for losing that part to Patsy, they could think again.

And if they thought that it made up for ignoring her like they did, well, they could give that some more thought too.

There was some discussion by a few of the more practical members of the class of what the duties of the vice president were and whether Nadia could do the job. Nadia sat there seething and listened to herself being discussed and wished she had never been nominated.

The children decided that the vice president should close the door during fire drills after everyone left the room. They decided she could do that, and just to make sure everything was all right, they would give her a "partner," the class secretary, to check up on her. Make sure she didn't get left behind or anything.

Then they voted and she was elected and she figured they all felt good, voting for the sick girl. A sympathy vote. After all, it was the right thing to do. And it didn't cause them any trouble. It didn't matter. It wasn't like it was a real vote.

When it did matter, like at recess or something, they didn't fool with her. They went off and played their games and left her alone, except when they got a touch of feeling sorry for her. Like when she came back to school after being out for two weeks in fifth grade—then they all wanted to play with her that day at recess. But there wasn't anything to play, so they just stood around for a while and talked and asked some questions, and the next day she was back under the tree by herself again.

| fourteen |

After lunch, Nadia waited at the top of the stairs with the class. She stood on her toes and stretched her neck high and peered out the window. Outside was stark and gray and windswept. Perfect Christmas weather, she thought. She had a warm coat and was dressed in layers, so the cold would not bother her. She wanted to go out.

She stood behind Carmalee Stoopenhall, the tallest girl in the class, and the oldest too, and hoped Mrs. Riley wouldn't see her there, but Nadia's trip to the sick room that morning had reminded Mrs. Riley what Mama's instructions were.

"Mrs. Beckley is keeping the recess group today, Nadia," Mrs. Riley said. "You too, Carmalee."

The recess group was the kids who had been bad. On rare occasions someone would have a cold and a note to stay in. And then there was Nadia, who stayed in when the weather was too hot or too cold or too wet, or any other time she had been feeling bad and had gone to the nurse.

Nadia dropped out of the line and followed Carmalee to Mrs. Beckley's door. She stood and watched the others heading outdoors. It wasn't fair.

Mrs. Beckley had a small group that day. Just Carmalee and Gunther Stoopenhall, plus an unknown boy working on math in the corner. And Nadia. Mrs. Beckley decided to leave them unsupervised while she went to the office for just a minute.

Nadia felt uneasy. Carmalee was a bad girl. She had a temper. You didn't mess with Carmalee. Everyone knew it. Carmalee and Gunther were holy terrors.

"Nadia, will you take names and write down anything they do, please?" Mrs. Beckley said.

Nadia didn't want that responsibility. "I ..." She tried to think of how to say no to a teacher, but Mrs. Beckley didn't wait around.

Carmalee took door-watch duty, and Gunther climbed up on the shelves by the windows. Carmalee ran out into the hall for water. Nadia wrote it all down, but Carmalee and Gunther couldn't have cared less.

Gunther jumped on top of the tables and sat at the teacher's desk. Carmalee, her only known skill being the ability to write like a grownup, changed the assignment on the board for Mrs. Beckley's class from examples 5–35 to examples 17–22. Nadia began to think Gunther and Carmalee were very funny, and she laughed until she doubled over, which pleased Carmalee and Gunther no end. They thought of other rules to break until the teacher returned.

"Any problems?" Mrs. Beckley asked.

Nadia looked at the list in her hand. She couldn't

remember when she had laughed so much. She didn't want to turn her list over to the teacher, but she figured she had to. She gave Mrs. Beckley the half-finished inventory of badness.

She would not look at Carmalee and Gunther because she knew they must be ready to kill, and anyway she already regretted what she had done. Then Carmalee and Nadia joined Mrs. Riley's line and went back to class.

"We'll get a beating for sure," Carmalee muttered in Nadia's ear.

Nadia turned around. The class had stopped by the water fountain.

"Beckley will give Ma and Pop a call, and we'll catch it then."

Nadia felt the sudden weight of unwanted responsibility. "I didn't know," she said.

"Not your fault, I reckon. Guess you don't never get whipped, do ya?"

"No," Nadia said.

"Maybe you could come over to my house one day, you reckon?"

Nadia thought about it. Mama wouldn't let her. She never went to see anyone, but she had thought about it. She had thought it would be fun. Of course she did not have Carmalee in mind.

"No, I guess not," Carmalee said, looking down at Nadia. She turned around and started punching the boy behind her in the line.

The Stoopenhalls were bad. But they were funny. And a friend. A real friend. Nadia wanted a real friend, even if it was Carmalee.

Nadia tapped Carmalee on the shoulder. "I'll ask my mother," she said.

That afternoon in class Nadia thought about going to Carmalee's house after school one day. Her. Sickly Nadia actually going to someone's house. And it wasn't some "invite the sick girl over and pretend to like her" situation, either. *Carmalee likes me because I laughed at her and Gunther,* Nadia thought. *She likes me because she thinks I like her and no one ever likes her.*

The tables were turned. Maybe Mama had not heard of the Stoopenhalls.

| fifteen |

They were late getting home that day. Nadia sat on the bottom step and blew on her hands to warm them while Mama searched for her keys in her pocketbook.

"A girl at school wants me to come to her house," Nadia said.

"Oh?" Mama looked up. "What girl?"

"Just a girl. You don't know her." Nadia stared out toward the woods through a thin gray mist. "Can I go?"

Mama pulled her keys from the purse. "Well, you know that might not be a good idea, Nadia."

No, Nadia didn't know that. Nadia thought it *would* be a good idea. She stood up, jammed her hands in her coat pockets, and stared up at Mama on the porch. "But I want to go," she said.

"I'm sorry, Nadia, but just look at those dark circles under your eyes," Mama said. "You can't go get all worn out after school at someone's house. You don't want to overexert yourself."

"I promise to only play sit-down games like cards. I *promise*."

"Nadia. You're already getting all worked up over this. Calm down now."

Mama put the key in the door, and Nadia listened to the old lock tumble. She buttoned her coat tight around her neck and stared back across the wintry haze that settled on the gardens.

"Nadia. Come in out of this cold and we'll get something to eat."

Nadia did not move. "You *have* to let me go!"

Mama came and put her arm around Nadia's shoulders. "I know you're disappointed. I'm sorry. Really, I am. Now won't you come on into the house? It's much too cold out here."

Nadia went inside. It was icy in the front hall, and they went to the kitchen, where it would be warm.

"What's the name of the girl?" Mama asked.

Nadia realized her mistake. She shouldn't have said a word about being invited to Carmalee's. The next thing Mama would be doing would be investigating. She might call up Carmalee's house. She might ask the teacher about Carmalee. Either way, it would not be good news.

"I don't want to go anymore," Nadia said. "She just feels sorry for me anyway. I hate her."

"You do not hate her, Nadia. I'm glad she wanted to be nice. And I'm sure she doesn't feel sorry for you."

"I still don't want to go," Nadia said. She saw that Mama looked satisfied. The argument was over, but she knew what she could do, and Mama didn't have to know a thing about it.

| sixteen |

It would be a lie. Nadia didn't like that, but she promised herself to play only safe, inside games, and she did need to get a friend before home school started, didn't she? So Mama wouldn't really mind, would she?

"I'm supposed to go see a girl in my class," Nadia told Aunt Lela on Wednesday afternoon. On Wednesdays, Aunt Lela picked up Nadia after school to watch her while Mama met with another home-school parent.

"What does your mama say?" Aunt Lela asked.

Nadia hesitated. "She says she's glad the girl wanted to be nice, and she doesn't think the girl feels sorry for me either."

"Well, fine then. I think it's a great idea. I've told your mother so many times that I think you should have friends."

Nadia handed Aunt Lela a crude map Carmalee had given her at school. Aunt Lela looked at it and laughed. "I think I can find that."

Carmalee was waiting on the front steps of a little house in the woods. She was twisting Gunther's arm behind his back. Nadia felt a little scared, but she went over to them. "We can't go inside," Carmalee announced. "Ma says so."

What kind of mother would make her kids stay out-side in the cold? Nadia felt uneasy. What would happen to her, having to stay out until Aunt Lela got back for her at five? This wasn't going right.

Carmalee watched Aunt Lela's car disappear down the dirt road. "That your ma?" she asked.

"My aunt," Nadia said. "She watches me on Wednesdays."

"*Watches* you? What's she watch you for?"

Nadia felt embarrassed. She didn't know what to say. Clearly no one ever watched these two.

"Come on." Carmalee started down the dirt road. Nadia walked beside her. She hoped it wasn't far, wher-ever they were going, because didn't Carmalee know she couldn't walk far?

Gunther followed behind with a long-legged black and white dog.

"Ever been to a sawdust pile?" Carmalee asked.

"No," Nadia said. They'd better get there soon or she'd have to stop.

"It's fun." Carmalee turned off in the woods where there had once been a road. Suddenly they were looking at a huge hill of old sawdust, maybe three times as tall as Nadia herself. "There it is," Carmalee said. "Come on!" She climbed to the top on all fours. "There used to be some kind of a sawmill or something here," she yelled down. "Come on up!"

The dog barked and tried the pile, but his thin legs

sank deep, and he lost interest and ran off in the woods. Gunther scrambled up, though, his feet making deep impressions in the brown sawdust.

It did look like fun. Nadia glanced around, already knowing that there was no one there to stop her. It might not be so tiring. She took a few steps. Her feet sank deep, and her shoes filled up with sawdust. Carmalee came rolling down the soft, mushy pile. Nadia climbed on. She felt like a mountain climber, and her feet felt all funny in her sawdust-filled shoes. She stood on the top. It was a strange feeling. She liked it. Gunther let loose with a whoop and slid down a steep side. Nadia laughed.

"Come on! Slide!" Carmalee yelled up at her.

Nadia was scared. "Mama will get mad. I'll mess up my school clothes," she said. She was glad she didn't have to say it was because of her heart. She shouldn't have climbed to the top in the first place, so she just stood there and watched them slide a few more times and imagined what it would be like.

Before long, they all stood on the cold ground and dumped the sawdust out of their shoes. The dog returned for the walk back to the house. Gunther wiped his runny nose on his jacket sleeve. Well, no wonder they had colds, Nadia thought. She hoped she wouldn't get one. She hoped there would not be serious repercussions from this whole episode. But Nadia stopped worrying long enough to laugh some more at Gunther's and Carmalee's sorry attempts at cartwheels on the road back. They looked so dirty she was glad she hadn't given in and slid down the sawdust pile herself. Then Mama would have known something was up for sure.

Back at the little house, Carmalee went to the side door and put her hands to the window, peering in. "Coast is clear," she said. She put up a finger for quiet and signaled for Nadia to follow.

They tiptoed into the kitchen. The TV made noise from behind a door. Carmalee grabbed a box of graham crackers from a cabinet and tiptoed through a little hall to her room. She closed the door and flopped onto her bed, reaching into the box of crackers. "Want some?" she said, offering Nadia the box.

Nadia took one. She pointed to a snapshot on Carmalee's mirror. "Are those your parents?" she asked.

"It's Grandpa and Grandma," Carmalee said. "They was nice people. They got killed in a car wreck. Pop, he says I'm the spittin' image of Grandma."

Nadia stared at the picture. Carmalee sat up and grabbed another handful of crackers. There was a tap on the window.

"Come on," Carmalee said, and she opened the window and tossed the box of crackers to Gunther, then climbed out, stepping down on an old sawhorse. Nadia followed. Climbing a sawdust pile *and* out a window. Like a real kid. No. Better than a real kid. Like some kid in a book or a movie or something.

Aunt Lela's car was there waiting. The afternoon had

flown by. Nadia got in the car. Her face was flushed, and she was smiling. "I had fun!" she yelled out the window at Carmalee and Gunther.

"Next time you come we can go down in the clay pit," Carmalee called back.

"Well, where did you go today?" Aunt Lela asked. She drove off, and Nadia watched Carmalee standing in the road, waving good-bye.

"The sawdust pile!" Nadia said. "They rolled and slid in it. I didn't. But Mama wouldn't like it that I went. So maybe you don't have to tell her?"

"Well, it's best to stay off those things," Aunt Lela said. "I've heard if they're old, the sawdust can rot out and make hollow places and you could fall down in it and get trapped, suffocated even."

Nadia's eyes were wide open. Wow! She would be sure to warn Carmalee about that at school.

| seventeen |

By the time they arrived at Aunt Lela's house it was raining. Nadia got out of the car and looked up into the clouds and watched the drops falling toward her, like when she was little and at the ocean with Daddy and Mama. They had sat in the warm, shallow waves, and the rain had come down, and they had laughed while Nadia held her face up and opened her mouth and tasted the raindrops.

"Come in out of that rain or your mother will have my hide," Aunt Lela called, so Nadia waited by the window watching for Mama, and when she got there, they drove into the country in silence. It had been a long day for both of them.

Nadia rubbed her cold hands together and looked out the car window. Winter fields spread back to a pine woods where a row of little white houses stood watch over the land.

Mama stopped at a store at the crossroads. "We need some bread. I'll be just a minute."

Nadia waited in the quiet, with only an occasional whisper of a car going by on the road. She felt unsettled about keeping the visit a secret. "Mama, I had fun," she whispered. But no. She could not tell. She had disobeyed.

She huddled up in her big hooded coat and waited in the silent car. It seemed too quiet, like home. Home was too quiet.

Out back of the store a dog barked. Nadia had a dog once. It was Daddy's dog, really. When Nadia was five and her daddy died, some people came one day and took Daddy's dog away, and she knew he would never come back either. The dog's name was Mac, and Mama said he had gone to live with those people now. Nadia had cried, and Mama had said Mac would be happier with the new people.

Nadia was too little to know why the dog went away, but now she knew. She had known for some time in the back of her mind. It made her mad. Mama sent the dog away. Mama didn't want him around anymore. Just another reminder of Daddy. But Nadia wanted the dog. Whenever she heard a dog bark, one she did not see, she would wonder, *Could it be Mac?*

At home, Nadia went to the front room to look for photos albums. There. On the lower shelf in the cabinet. She grabbed them and ran to her room to get warm, but she couldn't find a picture of Mac. She went back and looked in the cabinet again. She would just like to see their dog. Nothing else. Just Mac. What would be wrong with that?

Nadia found Mama washing dishes by the small

kitchen window. Rain fell through the black night and hit the panes, reflecting the flames from the heater.

Nadia stood with her hand still on the doorknob. "Mama, where are the other picture albums?" she asked. Careful not to say, *The one with pictures of Mac. And Daddy.* She would never say that. When Nadia was five she came home from school asking about her father. Mama's eyes welled up, and Nadia thought she had done something awful to make Mama sad. She didn't do it again.

"They should be out there in the front room," Mama said vaguely.

"They're not."

"Why don't you read a book, Nadia? You don't want to look at photos, do you?"

Nadia did want to see a picture of Mac, and another thought hovered almost without words. *A picture of Daddy, too.*

"There are only two albums out there," Nadia said. "I know there are more."

"Aren't they out there?"

Nadia waited before she answered. "No."

There was another silence.

"Why do you want to look at old photographs, Nadia?" There was an edge to Mama's voice.

Nadia pulled at her ponytail. She was in too deep.

"Well, supper's cooking," Mama said. "Why don't you read your new library book until then?"

Nadia got her book from the shelf, but she felt jumpy. Not ready to lose this round.

"This girl at school," Nadia said, "she has a picture of her grandparents, the ones who got killed in a wreck."

Mama looked at Nadia. "That must make her very sad."

"She didn't act sad."

"You don't know how she felt."

Nadia shut her mouth. She had gone to the forbidden topic. They weren't talking about Carmalee's picture anymore.

She opened her library book and looked back at Mama.

Mama knows where the pictures are.

But she didn't ask another time. The pictures would have Daddy in them. Mama didn't like to be reminded of him, because when he died, it completely broke Mama's heart. Aunt Lela had told Nadia.

Nadia's eyes were on her book, but her mind was on Daddy. He had died all of a sudden. It was his heart. Something was wrong, and the doctors didn't know it, and then he died. Nadia could feel her own heart pumping blood right then, and she wondered if she herself was a reminder to Mama. A reminder that Mama couldn't hide. A reminder that Mama could not give away.

| eighteen |

Thursday afternoon Nadia was outside the house in her coat and gloves. She hadn't told Mama she would be outside. She bet that Carmalee and Gunther and everyone else didn't have to tell if they went outside. But Mama would think it was too cold, especially with the sky so filmy and gray. Nadia stood under the arbor at the bottom of the steps and looked up through the tangle of bare wisteria vines.

When Mama discovered that Nadia was missing, she came to the porch. "What on earth?" she said. And then, "Nadia, your Aunt Lela just called."

Nadia kept looking up through the vines.

"She said you went to see a classmate yesterday. Why did you tell her I said you could go?"

"I didn't," Nadia said. She could tell that her mother was angry with her. A rare event.

"Well, that's the impression you gave."

"You said I shouldn't hate her. You said she was being nice to me."

"I told you no, Nadia."

Nadia turned her gray eyes toward her mother, and the wind blew her long, dark bangs across her pale face.

Mama wouldn't stay angry long. She wouldn't want to feel guilty for being angry with a poor sick child.

"Don't you ever try something like that again. Now come inside the house this instant."

Nadia plodded up the steps. She could tell Mama was still mad. Carmalee and Gunther would most likely get a beating for making their mother mad, but Nadia knew Mama wouldn't fuss at her much. Mama wouldn't want her to get all worked up and feel sick.

"And I know about the sawdust pile. What if you had fallen into it, Nadia?"

Nadia was horrified at the thought. Could that really happen? It had been fun. But now she knew. It had been a mistake.

She was glad nothing had happened, and she didn't want to think about it.

She went to her closet and got out the box of paper dolls and her copy of the school play. The parts were short and simple, and it wouldn't be long before Nadia would let the paper dolls do the whole play without looking at the copy.

She had a plan. If by chance some girl at school got sick the night of the play, she would take her place, because she would know all the lines.

| nineteen |

Mama was talking about home school again. Nadia thought it would be boring. Mama and Aunt Lela would be doing dull stuff about selling houses all day and sometimes Nadia would be left there with just that secretary.

Nadia stood toasting herself by the kitchen heater. *I will be alone*, she wanted to say, but how many times had Mama told her that home school would be perfect for her?

"It's too hot that close to the flames," Mama said. "Come sit down."

Nadia moved one step away from the heater.

Mama looked at her and sighed. "You must be tired," she said.

Nadia turned to toast her other side, moving closer again. Sometimes she heard Aunt Lela and Mama arguing. *Nadia should be around kids more*, Aunt Lela would say.

But Mama would say, *It just makes Nadia feel bad she's not like them.*

Maybe she's capable of more than you think, Aunt Lela would say.

Don't tell me about my child, Mama would say.

And sometimes Mama said, *If you had one of your*

own, maybe you'd understand. Then Aunt Lela would get mad. She wanted kids, but she never had any, and then she got divorced.

"Who are those children in our backyard?" Mama asked. She stood at the window over the wood bin and knit her brows. Nadia went to look.

It was Carmalee and Gunther. Carmalee had sneaked a note to Nadia that day in the recess group. It said that they were going to ride their bikes to Nadia's house and ask if she could go with them to the fair. They lived about three miles away from Nadia. Carmalee was making it up, Nadia thought. No one could ride three miles on a bike.

"Some kids from school," Nadia said.

Mama went to the back door and grabbed her windbreaker from the rack. "Stay right here. I don't want you out in the cold." She went out to the back porch and closed the door. Carmalee and Gunther were investigating the pump house. Mama went over to them, and Carmalee started talking. Carmalee looked almost as tall as Mama.

Gunther slipped in at the back door and stood in the hallway staring at Nadia. She followed his eyes as they gazed up the long staircase. "Cool," he said. "You got a room up there, I bet."

"No," Nadia said. There was a beautiful room upstairs she wanted. It would be fun to look down on the yard and woods from so high, but Mama thought she shouldn't be climbing the stairs all the time.

"This here house is big," Gunther mumbled, wandering down the hallway, peering into the kitchen.

"Your sister's waiting for you," Mama said. She stood behind Nadia and Gunther in the hall.

"Yes'm." Gunther pushed by her and disappeared onto the back porch.

Mama hung up her coat. Silence. Wasn't she going to say anything? Mama went into the kitchen. "Come on back in here where it's warm," she said.

Nadia followed her and sat at the table. She kept her eyes on Mama.

Mama's shoulders rose and fell. "Well, now I've met the girl you visited, and I guess you know what that was about. She wants you to go to the fair with her family tonight. Of course I explained to her that it was out of the question."

"But Mama, Carmalee said—"

"I don't want to hear what Carmalee said, Nadia, and I'm not angry with you. I'm sorry she had to come by here and get your hopes up like that when she doesn't know what she's talking about. It's just inexcusable that her parents would let her come over here like that. Surely the girl knew you are … a delicate child. I'll just be glad when you can leave that school and people like that, and this kind of thing will not be happening."

A disgruntled feeling crept into Nadia. It is true she had felt afraid of going to the fair when Carmalee was describing it at the lunch table, but at the same time, part of her did want to go. Very much. And Mama was saying no.

And it was more than that. Mama was putting her friends down, and it felt like Mama was putting her down too—for having such friends.

"I'm sorry I was cross, Nadia," Mama said. "It just came as a surprise. You should have told me what that girl was saying at school."

"I didn't think she'd come," Nadia said. "But can *we* go? You can take me."

"Oh, Nadia. They have dangerous rides and you have to do a lot of walking. There's nothing you'd like there." Mama stopped and gazed at Nadia, her eyes sad. "You wouldn't like it. I really am sorry, sweetie, but I'm thinking about what's best for you."

Nadia put her head down on the table. An angry tear crawled out of her eye.

"Now I should start supper," Mama said. "What would you like?"

"Toasted cheese sandwiches," Nadia mumbled at the wall.

"All right. Now cheer up, Nadia," Mama said. "Tonight we'll start a new book. It's a really good one."

Nadia went to her room and sat in her rocking chair. Blue and orange flames flickered in the gas heater, throwing a toasty heat her way. She *would* like the book. The books Mama picked for them to read aloud were wonderful, and it was fun to talk about them. Mama would call her when the food was ready, and she loved toasted cheese. But still ...

Tonight people would go to the fair, and Nadia thought Mama was wrong. There would be things at the fair she would like. The girls at the lunch table had told her things. Ferris wheels with lights. Cotton candy. But most of all, a magnificent carousel. They didn't have to tell her about that.

There were golden posts on carousels, and majestic horses, one dappled and gray with blue and red on the saddle. When Nadia was small, Daddy and Mama took her to a pavilion and she rode on the back of a gray dappled horse, gliding up and down and around so fast, so smooth, it was just like that horse was flying.

| twenty |

The paper dolls were put away now, back in their box on the shelf. The school play was learned, and anytime Nadia wanted, the dolls could put on the whole thing.

A winter sun, low behind the trees, cast a maze of shadows. Nadia stood on the front porch. She clutched her coat around her and listened to the undertone of wind in the pines. Being outside made her feel free. Even with her thoughts.

Nadia didn't talk about things that reminded her of Daddy. She didn't talk of Daddy at all. Sometimes, though, in spite of what Mama would think, Nadia thought of her father. Things reminded her. Straw grass, bending in the wind, golden in the late afternoon. Sandy roads, and long-eared dogs. Crisscrossed pine needles under the trees.

Nadia glanced back at the house. Mama was talking on the phone about software for home school. Let Mama find her missing. She'd show her. She'd show her it was all right to go outside like anyone else. She shouldn't care what Mama thought. And she didn't. Mama had a mean streak. Mostly she kept it hidden. Just like Mrs. Riley.

Nadia felt a little like being mean herself.

She took a road that curved through the woods down to a two-lane blacktop highway. She wished she could ride a bike and ride all the way to see Carmalee and Gunther.

Nadia heard a vague sound above the call of bob-whites and doves, and at first she wasn't sure it was really Mama. She turned around.

"Nadia!"

Mama *was* calling.

"Nadia?" There it was again. "Where are you?"

Nadia was almost to the bottom of the hill, but she wanted to go all the way to the highway. She hurried on, though the fun was gone now that Mama was scared. She stopped at the highway. Across the road there was a winter pasture, and at the far side tiny figures ran under a tree, circling, and she could barely make out their faint shouting.

Behind her, from the heart of the woods, she heard her name again, and the controlled fear in Mama's voice. Nadia was frightened by it.

Her eyes flicked back up the road. It curved into the woods. From the sound of the calls, Nadia guessed that Mama was running down that road toward her, flying down the uneven ground of the dirt road. Nadia saw Mama then, saw her trip, pick herself up, and run until she clutched Nadia by the shoulders.

Mama looked at Nadia, and Nadia saw that the fear was gone. Anger replaced it—anger at Nadia for making her scared. Mama's eyes were dark and angry, and all Nadia could think then was that her own eyes were gray.

Like Daddy's.

"What … are you doing?" Mama's words came in spurts as she tried to catch her breath. "What … why are you down here … why did you leave the house … without telling me? Why … what are you trying to do to yourself … to me?" Mama loosened her grip on Nadia's shoulders and let her arms fall limp. "Have you lost your mind, Nadia?" Her breath made icy puffs in the chilled twilight.

Nadia looked away. A car, just turning on its headlights in the oncoming dusk, hummed down the highway and disappeared over a hill, and a little part of Nadia wished she were in that car, going somewhere, not stuck here in this place where nothing could ever happen for her.

"Can't I even go for a walk? It's nice out here. I …" Her voice trailed off.

"I can't hear you," Mama said.

Nadia turned to her mother, her eyes down. "I feel trapped." Her eyes met Mama's. Her voice rose. "And I want a friend, and you won't let me do anything!" She had never shouted at Mama before, and now her chest felt funny. Tired.

Mama sighed. "You don't look well. Come on, you've got to get in out of this cold." She put her hand on Nadia's shoulder, but Nadia did not budge. "Nadia? Do you want to stay out here all night?"

No, Nadia did not want to stay all night, so she started

up the hill, and it was much too dark. She hadn't realized how soon it would turn dark. She felt drained. It was too hard to walk up the hill. She might black out. Her heart. Yes. It was throbbing. She stopped.

"I don't feel good," she whimpered.

Why hadn't she stayed in the house like Mama wanted her to? Mama was right about all of it. She should never have been mad at Mama. She crumpled forward to a little patch of moss under a tree and sat, her hand over her heart, feeling the pounding. It didn't feel right.

"Stay there!" Mama said, and ran into the darkness for the car.

A drizzle began, cold and wet, making the ruts in the road sloppy, like the tears on Nadia's face.

Don't let me die, God!

She tried to catch her breath. She studied her finger-nails. It was too hard to see in the dim light. Were they blue? Blue nails were supposed to be bad. They looked sort of purplish. Purple was red and blue. It was a bad sign. She had to stop crying. Her throat was too tight, and it seemed that she would wait there forever and that she might die there beside the road.

The wind came, scurrying about her in the dark, picking up leaves, stirring them in the air. They scattered in the wind, paper-thin leaves, wet and sticking to her face.

The doctor listened to Nadia's heart. He always listened to her heart. Every time. "I think you'll be fine," he said, and he talked to her mother in a hushed voice out in the hall. Her mother and the doctor talked, and she put it out of her mind as best she could, as she always did when her mother whispered with the doctor.

She used to think the doctor would help her. He sent her to a specialist in Charleston one time. She remembered the long ride down to the flat lowlands, the hours lying in the back seat of the car with the wind blowing in the window.

And when they came back, Mama asked the doctor to send Nadia to another specialist in Columbia, and Nadia knew that Mama was trying to find someone who could help. Nadia listened through the door and heard that doctor telling Mama there had been no need to make Nadia take that long trip. So Nadia knew there was nothing the doctors could do to make her well. She was not a baby. The doctor came back in and talked nicely to her, but she knew he was just being kind, and she was *not* fine, but that was not something you would say to a child.

Why did she go for that stupid walk down the hill and get herself into the doctor's office again? It was all her fault. She didn't want to think about it. She just wanted to go home and stop acting stupid.

| twenty-one |

Nadia was kept out of school on Monday to rest, but she wanted to go back on Tuesday. She sat in the back of the auditorium with a few other kids not in the play. They had moved to the corner to sit on the floor. She had been asked to play too. Carmalee had asked her. They played cards. Slapjack. Battle. Nadia had never had so much fun or laughed so much. And Carmalee and Gunther were teaching them a new game. Poker. It didn't last long, though. Mrs. Riley noticed they were gone and told them to sit up in the chairs so she could keep an eye on them.

Carmalee was different from the other kids, the ones who never asked Nadia to play. Carmalee was pushy. "Can I come over to your house one day?" she asked. "Ma says I can go. She says it's good I got a friend now."

Carmalee is like me, Nadia thought. *No friends.* And after the Christmas holidays Nadia would be home-schooled. There would be no more chances like this then for a friend.

"I have to ask Mama," Nadia said. "I'll ask her this afternoon."

"Can I invite Carmalee to the house this Saturday?" Nadia asked Mama as soon as she got in the car.

"Did you already talk to her about this?" Mama asked.

Nadia glanced at Mama. "*Yes.*"

"You shouldn't talk to her before asking me," Mama said. "I don't want the girl's feelings hurt. And don't use that tone with me, Nadia."

"She brought it up."

"I see."

Nadia watched the barren fields dotted with small, unpainted cabins. She watched a man bringing in some goats, their shadows long in the winter sun.

"Just explain that because of your health, you can't play like other kids, and so you can't invite them over," Mama said.

"We won't play stuff I can't do. We'll play cards."

"I don't think you want her for a friend. Someone else, perhaps."

Nadia's eyes flashed anger toward Mama, but Mama did not see. She reached over and patted Nadia's hand. "We'll work something out."

Nadia turned her face to the window. Some cows and an old tobacco barn swept toward her and then were gone.

"I'd love to be able to give you everything you want, and I'm sorry if you don't like my decisions, but it's for your own good."

"What's wrong with Carmalee?"

"For one thing, she's a troublemaker."

"What else?"

"Nothing else, except that her parents obviously let those children run wild, and naturally it must seem like fun to you. But I'm not sure her parents would fully understand about a child with special needs. And her brother just walked into our house without being asked. Who knows about those people?" She sighed. "Just tell the girl that you don't have kids over because of your health. She'll understand. I'll be glad to explain it to her again if you want."

"No." Nadia said. She had no intention of telling that to Carmalee.

On Wednesday morning, Nadia went to sharpen her pencils. Carmalee got in line behind her and asked, "What'd your mama say?"

"I didn't ask her," Nadia said. It didn't sound good. It sounded like she didn't care.

"Well. I wouldn't come anyway. We're getting new dogs, and we'll be too busy." Carmalee shoved in front of Nadia and sharpened her short pencil down to the quick. She pushed back past Nadia, elbowing her. "Sor-*ree*," she said. "It was a accident."

Nadia rubbed her arm and went back to her desk. Carmalee didn't have to be so ugly to her. After all, it wasn't her fault. It was Mama's. Not that Carmalee knew that. Nadia sighed. She didn't like talking about her heart. And she couldn't tell Carmalee that Mama didn't approve of her. What could she do?

Nadia was afraid to approach Carmalee at the back of the auditorium that day. She glanced, but Carmalee glared at her, so Nadia went and sat in the front. Eyes wide open, she watched the play, mouthing the words, and it was ridiculous, she thought, the way they kept forgetting. How were they going to get it right Friday night?

After play practice, Mrs. Riley needed a break. She took the whole class outside. No recess room for anyone.

Nadia stood alone under her tree. She watched the lonesome railroad tracks without their trains, and her eyes flicked sideways at the other kids from time to time. She told herself she would be glad when January came and Mama kept her out of this school. She would never have to stand here by herself like this again. She could not wait.

She picked at the bark around a hole in the trunk, pretending she didn't care. They were all mean. Even Carmalee. Well—maybe not Carmalee.

But if she just—please, please, please!—got her big break as the stand-in for someone in the play, everything would change anyway. Kids would be lining up to be her friend. Mama would be proud and surprised. She would want Nadia to have friends and to have fun. And you couldn't do that in home school. Home school would be off.

The closer the play got, the more jumpy Nadia became.

All week she recorded absences in her notebook. Friday would be crucial. That would be her big chance to stand in if someone was out. Every day that week, one kid was absent. But it had to be one of the kids in the play to count. It wasn't always someone in the play. Still, she had been polishing up those lines. She would be there Friday night. Ready.

| twenty-two |

Nadia figured that a teacher who would not even give her a little part wouldn't really want her to be the stand-in, but what choice would she have? It didn't matter, though. Friday night, no one was sick. They were all there and did the play, and Mrs. Riley had to whisper some of their lines to them from the front row so loudly that the audience could hear her, and everybody laughed, but then they all clapped and cheered and congratulated the players and made a big fuss over them for what a good job they had done.

And it wasn't a good job, Nadia thought.

Patsy's mother was especially proud of her, taking pictures of Patsy in her costume and bragging to everyone who came up to congratulate the "little star" about all the other things Patsy was great at too. And Patsy was proud of herself. Nadia could tell. Patsy hadn't forgotten her lines, but she said them in a put-on way that reminded Nadia of beauty contestants announcing their names in a pageant.

"That little black-headed girl did a real good job, didn't she?" Mama said when they left the school.

Nadia did not answer.

What was there to say? Mama would never believe that Nadia could have done a good job. Mama didn't know a thing about her *outstanding* tryout and what an *amazing* actress she was. Outstanding and amazing. And those were Mrs. Riley's words, not hers. Mama would never know, because Mama had made it clear from the first day that she did not want Nadia in that play any more than Mrs. Riley did, and it did not matter to them how *excellent* she was.

Nadia shivered a little inside her heavy coat. Sparkling Christmas trees glowed inside houses as they drove through town. She put her hand up on the window and watched.

When she got home that Friday night, she crawled into bed too jealous and angry and disappointed to sleep. She stared at the soft moonlight on the wall.

"Nadia?" Mama was at the door. She came into the room. "Are you feeling all right?"

"Yes," Nadia mumbled. But she wasn't. She wasn't feeling all right, and she knew exactly how she was feeling. Cheated. She felt cheated. Mrs. Riley had cheated her out of what should have been hers.

| twenty-three |

Mama told Nadia Saturday morning that she was going to invite Patsy over to see Nadia.

"No," Nadia said, but Mama went right ahead and did it anyway. Invited Patsy to play with Nadia. Invited her to play carefully with Nadia. Invited her to play with the sick girl. Not that Mama used those words.

Patsy was one of the girls Nadia had picked out as future friends that day she thought she would become the admired actress, the girl everyone wanted for their personal friend. But at tryouts Patsy had glanced at her with a look that said, *You think you stand a chance against me?!* And Patsy had whispered to her friends at the lunch table. Patsy was the queen of the sixth grade, and Nadia was no one.

Still, Nadia held out a little hope that morning when Patsy's mother brought her out to the house. Maybe Patsy remembered Nadia's admirable tryout and realized Nadia was worthy. They sat on the rug in the living room and played cards, and Nadia hoped it would be fun like that day with Carmalee and Gunther, but in the back of her heart she knew it wasn't.

It was staged, like Patsy in the play. She'd rather not

have Patsy over at all. She'd rather play with her paper dolls than Patsy. "Let's do something else," Nadia said, and she scooped up the cards.

Patsy was more than willing to stop. She wandered over to the window. "Too bad we can't go outside," she said.

Nadia grabbed her coat and turned piercing gray eyes on Patsy. "We *can* go outside," she said. "Come on."

Patsy followed Nadia out on the front porch and down the steps to the yard. "What can we do?" Patsy asked.

Nadia wrapped her scarf around her neck and put up her hood. "I'll show you around."

"You sure this is okay?"

"Why wouldn't it be?" Nadia said. So long as she wasn't going to go down the hill and then have to climb back up or anything else stupid.

"Well," Patsy said, "my mother said that she talked to your mother and you can't do a lot of stuff."

"I went to see Carmalee and we climbed up on a two-story-high sawdust pile," Nadia said. "Your mother is wrong."

"She is not!" Patsy said.

"Well, she must be." Nadia stomped off around to the back of the house. "I'll show you the barn. It's real old. People used to keep animals in it." They walked back through the vine arbors, now bare and casting lacy shadows on their faces.

Nadia and Patsy stood in the wide barn door looking.

"Hey," Patsy said, "there's a big haystack in there. Let's slide on it."

"No," Nadia said.

"Why not?"

"It's not safe in there. No one's allowed to go in. There's rotten boards." Nadia knew the rotten boards weren't what was keeping her out of there.

"Well, what *can* we do?" Patsy said, following Nadia back to the front steps and sitting beside her. "What do you do? Besides play cards."

"Well, I read books. And play board games. And I do plays."

"What do you mean?"

"Well, I make them up about shows I see. I act them out, and I do all the parts."

"Okay," said Patsy. "Let's do that."

"Let's do the play from school." Nadia stood up. "The porch will be the stage. You do your part and I'll do all the others. Unless you know some of the others and then we'll decide."

"You know the parts?" Patsy said.

"I know 'em all," Nadia said. "I wish the teacher had let me have a part. I wouldn't have forgotten the lines. Mrs. Riley makes me sick."

"Mrs. Riley didn't do anything," Patsy said.

"She chose people who forgot their lines, and I didn't forget anything in my tryout. I used to think she was nice, but not anymore."

"It's not Mrs. Riley's fault," Patsy said.

"Go ahead and stick up for her 'cause she chose you for Christina. It is so her fault. She's the one who chose."

"You're jealous." Patsy stood up and pulled her hat down over her ears. "You think you know so much." She glanced toward the house and stuck her hands in her jacket pockets.

Nadia glared at Patsy. "I think *you* know nothing."

"Oh, really. It was your mother who said not to pick you for the play."

"She did not. She didn't even know I was trying out."

"Well, she knew there was a play. She came by after school on my day to wash the boards. Your mother told Mrs. Riley that she didn't want you to do any of the parts because it would be too stressful, and you had to be careful because of your bad heart. And Mrs. Riley said what about the Little Theatre group you were in, and your mother said you weren't in any Little Theatre group."

Nadia turned away and kicked at a pebble so Patsy would not see her face. *Mama told Mrs. Riley not to pick me?*

"Mrs. Riley *told* your mother you had done a good tryout. She would have picked you for something if your mother hadn't stopped her."

"For something. In other words, not for your part," Nadia said.

"I didn't say that!"

"I don't want to do this anymore," Nadia said. She sat down on the steps. "It's too cold."

Patsy stood watching her.

Nadia knew what she was thinking. *Pitiful sick girl.*

Nadia got back up and went to the front door. She turned back. "You need to call your mother. I have to lie down now," she said. She ran inside to her room and slammed the door. The flames jumped in the gas heater.

She sat in her rocking chair and wrapped her arms around herself. The rocking soothed her, and she watched the flames. So Mama was afraid Mrs. Riley would give her a part. So Mama snuck around behind her back and made sure it would not happen.

And all that time I was learning the part and thinking I had a chance.

Her door opened. "Sweetie?" Mama said. "Patsy says you feel sick."

"I don't like her," Nadia said. "I want her to go home." Nadia wanted Mama to leave too. Leave her alone. She wanted to think. She needed to figure out what had just happened. She grabbed her book from the table and opened it, pretending to read.

"I'll just go wait with Patsy then," Mama said. "If you're sure you're all right."

"Well, I *am!*"

"Don't get all excited, Nadia."

She *was* all excited. She would be excited if she

wanted. The door clicked shut. She pushed a chair in front of the door to keep Mama out. There must be a key somewhere. If only she could find it. Nadia sat on the floor and slapped her paper dolls out on the rug. She smoothed out a small tear on one doll's neck. She frowned. The dolls smiled.

Paper dolls. Paper books. Paper cards. Paper life.

She took a deep breath. The paper dolls lay on the rug. Smiling.

Paper friends.

After Daddy died, Nadia found out about her heart. Nadia thought it was like paper. Like having a heart made out of paper. She learned to be afraid. To be careful. If she wasn't careful her heart might tear.

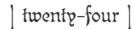

| twenty-four |

The soup on the stove began to boil, and Mama put the cheese sandwiches in the oven.

"What happened with Patsy?" she asked.

Nadia didn't know what she wanted to say yet. She picked up the saltshaker, a little blue earthenware pig, and rolled it around in her hands. She put her head down on the table and sat the little pig in front of her eyes.

"Nadia?"

"What?" Nadia said.

"Did Patsy say something to upset you?"

Nadia stood the little blue pig in her hand and stared at it. She kind of liked this game. Her with the secret. Mama guessing.

"You're mad at me for asking Patsy to see you, is that it?" Mama asked.

"No."

A tiny stream of cold found its way through the window frame beside the kitchen table. Nadia glanced at Mama. Mama was pretending to have lost interest, but Nadia knew she was still curious. Well, Mama could just not know what was going on for a change.

Nadia was still sulking after lunch. Brittle grass crunched beneath her feet, breakable as her heart. She was bundled in her hooded coat in the brisk wind that whipped across the hard winter earth, away from the house, at the edge of the pines. She watched the branches bend in the gray winter sky and heard the whisper of cold air through their needles.

It felt like Christmas. This coming Friday was the day school got out for the holidays. The day Mama would take her to pick out a tree. The night they would decorate it. She wasn't ready for Christmas. She was too angry for Christmas.

Mama sat inside with her newspaper. She hadn't asked any more about what was upsetting Nadia, so Nadia stood outside where Mama would think it was too cold to go, and where without bothering to ask Mama she had gone anyway, so that Mama would know how angry she was without her saying a word, because she didn't have the words. So Mama could find her here, and then Mama would know.

Nadia's toes began to hurt with the cold, and her nose got red, but she stayed, and finally Mama came and called from the porch for her to come in at once, but not until Mama came down into the yard to her and asked her what she was doing did she go back to the house.

| twenty-five |

Mama left Nadia in the kitchen, but Nadia crept into the hallway and listened. "May I speak to Dr. Smith?" Mama was saying.

"No," Nadia cried. She ran in and pushed down the buttons under the receiver. "Why are you calling him?" she screamed. She grabbed the receiver from her mother's hand and hung it up. "It's not about the doctor. It's about *you*! Patsy told me. I could have been in the play, but you ruined everything!"

Mama looked relieved. "So that's what this is all about. You didn't tell me you wanted a part in the play."

"How could I tell you, Mama, when you told me I didn't want it? I was going to be an actress. Not just the sick girl. That's all I am at school, you know. I learned the tryout and I thought I would win!" Nadia was shouting. She felt faint. She wasn't used to shouting. "You never asked me what I wanted! You *told* me I didn't want to do it." She lowered her voice. "You told me what I was supposed to *think*. And you took it away from me, too! You told Mrs. Riley not to let me have that part. You told her not to let me have any part."

Her words were no good. There were no words to make Mama understand. And now her chest felt tight.

"Nadia, I have to make hard choices. I have to do what's best for you."

She knew Mama would say that. How could you argue with that? She might as well have said nothing. She sat down on the floor, her hand over her heart, pressing over her heart. She rocked slowly back and forth. "I hate you!" she said, her voice quiet, afraid to say it. Her heartbeat thumped in her neck. "I don't feel good."

"I'm calling the doctor," Mama said.

"No!" Nadia wiped her eyes and sniffled. "I don't want to go. He can't do anything!" She swallowed. "I feel better now."

It was a lie. She did not feel better.

Mama stared at her, hesitating, the phone in her hand. "You feel better? Really?"

"I don't want to go!" Nadia shouted. Mama put the phone down, but Nadia knew that the minute her back was turned Mama would call the doctor.

"Come lie down on the sofa," Mama said. "I'm going to make you some hot chocolate."

So Nadia lay under a quilt and felt better, and Mama went to make the chocolate. Nadia knew Mama had called the doctor from the other room.

It frightened her, getting so angry with Mama that she had lied about feeling better when she really didn't. She vowed not to ever do that again, because if she had really needed the doctor, it would have been too late. Like with Daddy.

| twenty-six |

Mama panicked. Something perhaps that Mama saw in the way Nadia looked during the argument. Or after the argument. When she brought Nadia the chocolate. It made Mama panic, and that made Nadia frightened. Mama put her in the car for the twelve-mile drive to the hospital. When Mama panicked, she drove fast. It wasn't the first time, and it frightened Nadia even more than Mama's alarm.

"Slow down, Mama," she said. But Mama wasn't listening. "You're going too fast," Nadia said. "We're going to get in a wreck."

"We've got to get there," Mama said. "It's going to be okay." She started to pass a car, but a truck was coming.

"Don't do that!" Nadia screamed, but Mama pulled into the other lane. There was no room to pass, and nowhere for anyone to go. Big lights. A horn was blowing. Mama swerved back into her lane. Out of control. It was all spinning. Sliding. Hitting things.

And then stillness.

It couldn't have been long, just a few seconds, before a branch broke in the quiet. More branches. Snapping. Someone with a flashlight. Mama said something. And Nadia heard her own voice. Weak little cries.

The car was off the road in the woods, and it kept getting colder and colder while they waited for the ambulance. Mama was pleading with her, asking if she was all right, and Nadia hurt all over and cried loudly, but she would not let Mama touch her.

Mama had almost killed her! Almost killed them all! The people in the other cars. Everyone.

She pushed Mama away. "Get away," she screamed.

Other faces were there next to Mama's, looking at Nadia where she sat in the car. Nadia was embarrassed by her own yelling. She turned her face away. Blood was caked in her hair and trickled down her face. She wiped it away and stared at it. It shocked her.

They were lucky, the doctor said. All they needed was stitches. And the people in the other cars were not seriously hurt either. It could have been much worse.

Aunt Lela came and got them. They would spend the night at her house. Mama would have to get a car to use while hers was being repaired. Nadia was excited about spending the night away from home. There was a sense of well-being now that they knew everyone would be okay. Aunt Lela was fixing them a sandwich to have in front of the TV. It would be fun.

"You need to go right to bed," Mama told Nadia.

Nadia sat in a big rocking chair in Aunt Lela's den. "I want to watch TV," she said. She kept rocking. "I want the sandwich, too."

"I'll bring it to you. Staying up after all that you've been through would not be good for you. I talked to the doctor. Now, off to bed."

Nadia frowned. "What did he say?"

"You need your rest, Nadia."

Nadia trudged off to the guest room and put on the fresh nightgown Aunt Lela had left out for her to wear. It was too big, and she laughed at how long the sleeves were. She slipped under the covers. She was not sleepy. Why did Mama have to ruin the visit at Aunt Lela's?

Mama brought the sandwich in, saw the long sleeves that covered Nadia's hands, and rolled them up for her. Nadia sat up and started eating. The lamp cast warm colors around the room.

Mama sat on the edge of the bed. "You know, Nadia, we were going to start your home schooling right after New Year's, but I've decided to go ahead and take you out of school now. This accident. The way you got so upset about … well, all that school business about the play. The children there."

"But I was supposed to stay until after the class party. I'll miss the Christmas party!"

"You've had a very traumatic experience tonight, Nadia. I won't be sending you back for a while anyway. It makes sense to go ahead and start the home schooling. You'll like it. Just think—you'll have more time to spend on things you enjoy, like reading. Won't you like that?"

Nadia took another bite.

"You won't waste time doing busywork like you do in school."

"But the party. Can't I—"

"Nadia, you don't want to get all worked up again and start feeling bad, do you?"

No. She did not. She finished the glass of milk on the tray and cuddled down under the covers. She would not say anything about it. She would not think about it. She did not want her heart to start acting up again.

That accident was Mama's fault.

She would not think about that either.

"This is going to be a good thing, Nadia," Mama said as she turned out the light and left Nadia there under the covers with her eyes wide open in the dark.

| twenty-seven |

The pain in Nadia's chest was new. It woke her early Sunday in Aunt Lela's guest room, and she called out for Mama.

"It's my *heart*," she screamed. Aunt Lela came running then and drove them to meet Doc Smith at his office.

But it was not her heart, Doc Smith said. It was pulled muscles from the car accident. Maybe even a hairline fracture in a rib. She would be fine.

Nadia did not believe him. She could hear the dread in Mama's voice. She could see the terror in Mama's eyes. Something awful had finally happened to her.

"I'm going to talk with your mother a minute," Doc Smith told Nadia. "You wait with your aunt out front."

Nadia didn't trust him. What did he have to say to Mama that he couldn't say in front of her? She started down the hall, but when the door of his office closed, she stole back again. Her chart lay on the table.

They didn't need to treat her like a baby. It wasn't like she didn't know anything. Why shouldn't she know what he was telling Mama right now? It was *her* heart. She narrowed her eyes, and angry tears plopped out. Her hand touched her chart, and she glanced back to the hallway. If she was quick, they would not catch her.

It was cold in the house. The heat had been turned off right before they left Saturday for the hospital. Before the accident. Before staying at Aunt Lela's and before Nadia came face to face with her chart.

"Come on, Nadia, let's read a new book," Mama said. Nadia went to Mama's room and sat on the couch in front of the heater.

You do not know what I saw.

Mama lit the heater. "Did you see the books I got?"

Nadia didn't know how to act or feel. She picked up two new books from the couch. "These?" she asked.

"Which one do you think we should start with?"

Nadia looked at the covers. She had looked already, but she didn't say it. Both books appealed to her. She didn't say that either. She didn't talk about the covers. She didn't do any of the things she usually did. She just stared at the books in her hand.

"Do you want me to pick?" Mama said.

"Okay."

Mama started reading, and Nadia pushed the baffling thoughts away. All the time that Mama was checking on car repair and getting a rental, and all the way home, Nadia had wondered about the chart.

She didn't want to think about it anymore. Now all she wanted was for Mama to be Mama again.

The book was about a girl Nadia's age, and soon Nadia was caught in the story. She leaned closer to Mama, drawing her legs up on the couch and getting comfortable. She stared into the flames and thought about the story, and Mama read on.

After three chapters, Mama closed the book. "Well, that's where we'll stop for now," she said. "I'm going to go get lunch started."

Nadia hobbled to the window, still sore from the accident. The words came back.

Dec. 14. Slight bruising and pulled muscles over rib cage. Possible slight rib fracture. Exam otherwise normal.

Outside, the wind blew dried leaves around the grape arbor where they picked tons of scuppernongs in the summer.

Dec. 13. Stitches needed on scalp wound. Mother reports patient was feeling bad prior to car accident. Probable panic attack following argument with her mother.

So many scuppernongs that they would take bowlfuls to people Mama knew.

Dec. 6. Normal exam. Slight functional heart murmur unchanged. The child's mother has been assured again that it is not serious.

Nadia had searched back and back through heights, weights, shot records, and measles.

Specialists agree the child's heart is normal with only a minor functional murmur. Her mother appears overly concerned, but I have reassured her of our findings.

So.

She did not have a bad heart.

Her heart was fine. She could run like anyone else, and she felt like she could fly!

But all these years had been a lie. Mama telling things that only Mama believed.

Telling everyone.

While the doctor didn't know what Mama was saying to people.

While Nadia stood under the tree like a fragile egg instead of a girl.

Mama appeared back at the door. "The soup is cooking."

"I saw my chart," Nadia said. "I went back and looked at it."

"You what?" Mama came into the room. "You … read …?"

"Why did you tell me I had a bad heart, Mama?"

There it was again. In Mama's eyes. Fear. Mama wasn't deliberately lying. Mama was truly afraid. It was crazy.

"You have a murmur, Nadia."

"But the chart says it's not serious. And those other doctors you took me to, they said so too."

"Doctors are all the same, Nadia. You know how bad you feel. Your father had some bad feelings too. Did you know that? Do you know what the doctor said about your father?"

"No."

"The doctor said it was nothing."

What Mama said made Nadia feel sick. Mama thought the doctor was wrong about her too.

She looked at her fingernails like Mama did sometimes. Not that Mama ever said the real reason she was looking. Instead she'd say that she wanted to see if Nadia was biting them. But Nadia knew Mama was looking at the color. Nadia's nails were dull, not the bright pink she'd noticed on other kids.

Nadia rubbed her thumbnail, trying to make it pinker. *No.* She would *not* think like this. Mama was wrong to make her start thinking like this. She would *not* go into a panic. She did not have to panic anymore. She believed her chart.

She took a deep breath and blew it out slowly. Like Mama had told her to do many times. To calm down. She glanced back at Mama.

Take a deep breath, Mama.

How could Nadia stop the panic for Mama when words from the doctor meant nothing to her? Would people think she was crazy? Would they send her away somewhere? If anyone found out.

Nadia could not tell anyone. Ever. She didn't want Mama sent away.

Mama gave her a hug. "You are going to be just fine if you do what I say. I won't let anything happen to you."

Nadia had nothing left to say.

| twenty-eight |

Nadia started home school at Mama's office on Monday. She still hurt a little from the accident.

But my heart is fine.

She had to keep reminding herself.

And she told Mama she felt okay.

The office was as boring as when she did homework there after school. Mama explained pages in the English and math books. Nadia showed her displeasure by looking around at the ceiling and saying it was too much and that she did not like English and math.

"It is no more than you would have at school," Mama said. "Now don't act spoiled, and I'll let you choose where we go for lunch."

Nadia made a production of getting out paper and putting it in her notebook and sharpening several pencils until Mrs. Branch brought typed letters for Mama to sign and said clients were waiting. Then Nadia moved to her homework table in an unused room of shelves and file cabinets near the back door.

She wrote her name at the top of her paper, but there was no reason to do that. Mama knew who her only student was. Nadia erased it. After working five math problems, Nadia put down her pencil and stared out the window at a parking lot behind the corner gas station.

It was a cage. Mama had put the fragile egg-child in the cage so she could be watched for breakage.

But I will not break.

And she had wanted to make decorations with the class. With glitter and colored paper and tinsel. She put her head down on her table out of habit, but there was no June telling Mrs. Riley that Nadia was acting sick.

The kids probably don't even notice I'm gone.

Yet Nadia was disappearing. Already. And here it was just the first day. Her desk at school was empty. After Christmas they'd move it out of the room. Someone would say, *What happened to Nadia?* And another would say, *Who?* Nadia would go back and forth from the storage room to the house. Only Mama and Aunt Lela and a few real-estate grown people would ever see her. No one her age would see her.

At least under the tree she was a shadow in the distance. Here, she was nothing.

She could not stay here just because Mama would feel better with her here.

No more.

The kids are going to know there is a girl named Nadia.

She kept an eye on her watch, and at eleven o'clock she went to Mama's office. "Your mom's gone to show the Barker house to some people from Darlington," the secretary told her.

Nadia gave her a vacant look. "I know," she said. She went back to her homework room.

Dear Mama,
    I think I will just go on back to my class this week, until the holidays at least, since that is what you had always said. Home school would start after Christmas. It is boring here.
        Nadia

She read it over. That should suit Mama for now. Surely Mama would leave her alone about school for one week.

She typed the next letter on an old word processor.

Dear Mrs. Riley,
    Nadia may play outdoors at recess from now on.
        Dr. Smith

She packed her books. The school was six blocks down Home Avenue.

| twenty-nine |

"Nadia!" Mrs. Riley said. "I thought you were starting home school today."

"Not until after the Christmas party on Friday," Nadia said. She went to her desk and did the same math page she had started that morning. If she had to do problems, she would rather have company.

She was sprinkling her Christmas star with a generous portion of glitter when she was called to the office to talk to her mother. Mama had phoned to make sure she was okay after that walk to school, and Mama was angry, but she gave in about letting Nadia stay when Nadia whined about the glitter. Nadia went back to class. She was on her way to being the *new* Nadia. Things were going well. Glitteringly well, she told herself. And she was full of ideas about getting around Mama. But she should not have whined. She wanted to stop that. After all, she decided, the *new* Nadia should not whine.

Nadia stopped in front of Carmalee's desk. Carmalee shot her a dagger with her eyes.

"I just wanted to say I should have told you the truth to start with," Nadia began.

"*What* are you talking about?"

"Well, my mother says I'm too sickly to have kids over ... unless she picks them out first and makes sure we don't have any fun. But I'm not sickly anymore anyway."

Carmalee eyed Nadia.

"You'll see. And I can play at your house, but it has to be when I'm visiting my aunt. If you're not mad anymore."

"Well," Carmalee said. "*Okay.*"

Nadia stood there a moment.

"What now?" Carmalee said.

"I need a favor."

"Yeah?"

"Since you can write like a grownup, will you sign Dr. Smith's name on this note?"

Carmalee sat up tall. This was a compliment. She did not get compliments. "Sure. And since we're friends, I won't charge you for it."

Nadia slipped the note on Carmalee's desk.

"What's his first name?" Carmalee asked.

"I'm not sure. Just write 'Dr. Smith.'"

When Carmalee was through, Nadia admired the results. She held on to the note until it was time for recess, and then she took it to Mrs. Riley. When she got in line she saw that Mrs. Riley was looking at her. *Seeing me like a normal girl now,* Nadia thought.

 | thirty |

Carmalee was in the recess group, so Nadia approached Patsy, Bethy, and Lindsey out on the playground.

"Why are you outside?" Patsy asked.

"I'm better. I can do stuff now," Nadia said.

The girls looked at each other. "I thought you were friends with Carmalee and her stupid, ugly brother," Patsy said.

Nadia frowned at them.

"Well, they're staying in," Lindsey said. All three girls laughed.

"Why are you friends with them anyway?" Patsy asked.

Nadia hesitated. She wanted to be popular. "Who said I was?" A bad feeling crept into her stomach.

"You did. You said it when I was at your house. You'd been to their house and done something stupid like climb a dirty old sawdust pile."

Nadia stared at them. Why were they being so mean? This wasn't the way it was supposed to be.

She turned away and walked to her old tree. They would see. It would be different. Soon she would always be out here acting like everyone else and then those horrid girls would see. They probably thought she was making it all up. She didn't care. They weren't the only kids around here. They were mean. She didn't want to be friends with them anyway.

She hated them.

She saw Mrs. Beckley watching the classes. Then she panicked. What if Mrs. Riley didn't believe the note? What if Mrs. Riley was inside calling her mother right now? Her mother would not answer. Her mother was supposed to be showing houses all day today. Would Mrs. Riley call Doc Smith?

What would he say? *Yes, Nadia can go out and play,* Doc Smith would say. *By all means.*

Well, I'm just checking, Mrs. Riley would say. *After all, she has always been so sickly.*

She's never been sickly, Doc would say. That was what he would say. Her heart sank.

Well, her heart and all, Mrs. Riley would go on. *She's never been able to play like the others.*

Tell me what you're talking about, Doc Smith would say.

No! That wasn't the way it should go. No. It wouldn't happen like that, would it?

Nadia was already running across the playground.

It could happen like that. It could. She would have to stop Mrs. Riley from calling. If Mrs. Riley said anything like that, then Doc Smith would find out what all Mama had been telling people. About how Mama had raised her.

Nadia had a pain. She stopped and held her side. What was happening? She ran up the steps, in the door, more steps, and her side was hurting. What was wrong now? She wasn't supposed to be sick.

She had to stop Mrs. Riley. She passed the second-grade rooms and pushed open the door to the office. Mrs. Riley was hanging up the phone. Looking over at her. Nadia stared back and held her side and tried to catch her breath.

"Did you—call him yet?" she said. But she could tell. By the look on Mrs. Riley's face.

Yes. She had called.

And yes. It had pretty much gone the way Nadia had just imagined.

| thirty-one |

Nadia would stay with Aunt Lela while Mama was away. Mama had emotional problems. Mental problems. Mama could not stop thinking Nadia was sick like her father had been, even when the doctors explained that it was not at all the same thing. So Mama was at a fancy rest home out in the country where people would work with her on getting better. On getting over her fear.

Mama had the problems, but Nadia would have a counselor to talk to also. Nadia didn't want to. It was Mama who needed help. Doc Smith had talked to Nadia. "Sometimes you might still be afraid of normal things," he told her. He knew kids who really *were* sick who did more than she'd been allowed to do. And her feelings toward her mother. These were things Doc Smith thought Nadia needed to talk about.

She stood in a sunroom full of plants with Aunt Lela. It was where Mama was getting help. When Mama came in, Nadia glanced at her and then turned her head away.

"How are you feeling?" Mama asked.

Nadia shrugged. She wanted to scream, *Why are you still asking how I feel?*

"Nadia, I want you to know that I'm realizing I've done things wrong."

Nadia stared out at the woods. She did not believe Mama. She wished she had not come here.

"Nadia?" Mama said.

"What?"

"I'll be here for a few weeks at least, before we can go back home together, but I'm going to be coming up to Lela's for Christmas to see you. Did you know that?"

"Yes," Nadia said, still looking outside. Aunt Lela had told her that.

"Let me give you a hug," Mama said.

Nadia didn't know what to say or do, so she stood still while Mama hugged her. She wanted to yell at Mama. She wanted to bring her box with the pictures of Daddy and Mac. She had found them where Mama had hidden them. She wanted to shove them in Mama's face. She wanted to say, *I've taken these. You didn't want them, and you didn't want me to want them, but I do, and they are mine now.*

Aunt Lela had told Nadia that she might not understand why her mother had told everyone she was sick. Aunt Lela was wrong. Nadia was not a little kid. She knew what had happened. After Daddy died, Mama panicked when the doctor found Nadia's heart murmur, afraid it was serious. She couldn't get it out of her head. She was controlled by her fear. Mama blamed the doctors for what happened to Daddy. She would not let it happen again.

Nadia understood, but she was mad. Aunt Lela and Doc Smith said she would be angry. They were right about that. She wandered to another window and stared out. She didn't want to listen to them talking, and she was glad she wasn't staying long.

She ran ahead to get in Aunt Lela's car, and when she and Aunt Lela drove away, Nadia looked back and saw Mama standing in a small outdoor garden, watching them. All of a sudden Nadia felt sorry for her. She waved, but Mama didn't seem to see as she stood in the bright sun, her hand shielding her eyes, frowning after them. Nadia wanted Mama to see her, to know she wasn't still angry. She waved again, leaning out the window until Mama saw and smiled and waved back.

| thirty-two |

The temperature was below freezing outside. Mrs. Riley let her class go out anyway, hoping to calm them down before the party.

Nadia stood bundled in her parka in the middle of the playground. The wind swept around her legs, stork thin despite two pairs of knee socks, and sand twirled in little drifts on the hard-packed ground. She looked for Carmalee, but Mrs. Riley was still talking to her. So Nadia waited.

Suddenly a group of girls surrounded her. She fixed her pale, dark-circled eyes on them. Doc Smith said it was just her natural coloring, those dark circles. She had asked.

Nadia squinted at the girls, looking at one and then another. Now she was free to become one of them.

The girls wanted to know why Nadia's aunt brought her to school these days. They wanted to know where her mother was. Did she have to answer all their questions to be their friend?

Well, her mother was this very night coming to Aunt Lela's until after Christmas. And they were all going to get the tree and decorate it. She had phoned Mama when she got home the other day from the visit, and they had made the plans. She was glad they had that place for Mama. Mama would get better there.

"Cat got your tongue?" Lindsey asked.

"No."

"Well?"

"Well what?"

"Are you going to tell us?"

"Maybe."

"Oh! Look, y'all," Patsy said. "There's Nadia's big old stupid friend." The others laughed.

Carmalee was following the fence at the edge of the playground. Her ratty tweed coat swallowed her. Her eyes were squinted against the icy wind. She looked mad. Nadia knew what they expected her to say now. Carmalee was stupid. And bad. And that she was *not* her friend.

But all of a sudden Nadia knew. She didn't have to answer their questions. She didn't have to think what they thought. She didn't have to say what they wanted her to say. She wasn't that friendless girl standing under trees.

"You're right," Nadia said. "About Carmalee being my friend. And, well, since y'all are so curious about my family, I'm visiting my aunt. My mother and I both. We'll be there at Christmas."

And Nadia knew she didn't want to stand there with that group of girls. She looked out over the school grounds. Carmalee was near the old tree. Nadia glanced back at the group. "I'll see y'all later," she said, and she walked off.

She stopped when she got to the giant oak and put her hands on the trunk. Everything was just as she had left it, but it seemed so long ago that she had stood there. Gray tangles of Spanish moss trailed from the branches in the cold December air, and a train rattled by down past the bluff.

She remembered standing there, wishing for trains to come by. When they did, she didn't feel quite so lonely. Well, she didn't need to wish for trains now.

Carmalee glanced her way and started running off.

"Hey," Nadia called, "wait for me!"

She ran after Carmalee toward the ballfield. There was a group of children gathering there. Nadia ran on to catch up, feeling strange to be running, but strong, and when she got to the field she could barely hear the sound of the train.